Conor's
Cowboy Suit

GILLIAN PERDUE
•Pictures by Michael Connor•

THE O'BRIEN PRESS
DUBLIN

First published 2002 by The O'Brien Press Ltd,
20 Victoria Road, Dublin 6, Ireland.
Tel: +353 1 4923333; Fax: +353 1 4922777
E-mail: books@obrien.ie
Website: www.obrien.ie
Reprinted 2002.

ISBN: 0-86278-778-5

British Library Cataloguing-in-Publication data
Perdue, Gillian
Conor's cowboy suit. - (O'Brien pandas ; 23)
1.Children's stories
I.Title II.Connor, Michael
823.9'2[J]

2 3 4 5 6 7 8 9 10

02 03 04 05 06 07 08 09 10

The O'Brien Press receives
assistance from

thearts
council
schomhairle
ealaíon

Typesetting, layout, editing and design: The O'Brien Press Ltd
Illustrations: Michael Connor
Printed by the Woodprintcraft Group Ltd

Can YOU spot the panda
hidden in the story?

Conor loved cowboys.
He knew all about them
from books and TV.

Cowboys rode horses
across the dusty plains.

They threw their lassoes
and shouted:
'Yee haw! Giddy-up!'

They slept in tents
and sang songs
around the campfire.

But what Conor loved
most of all
was their **clothes**.

He loved the big, shady hat
that kept the sun
out of their eyes.

He liked the little scarf
that they wore in a knot
around their necks.

If there was a dust storm,
the cowboy would pull
the scarf over his
mouth and nose
to keep out the dust.

They wore jeans, of course,
and cool waistcoats.

And they had
funny leather trousers
called 'chaps'
that they wore
over their jeans.

Cowboys wore big boots
with spurs sticking out the back.

And, best of all,
they had a gunbelt
with two holsters for their
two shiny guns.

Every day
Conor played cowboys.

Every night he dreamed of
being a cowboy.

He drew pictures of cowboys
and coloured in
all their clothes
very carefully.

Then one day
a great thing happened.

Mum and Dad got Conor
a very special present.
It came in a huge box.

The box was wrapped
in paper and was sitting
on the kitchen table.

Mum and Dad
and big sister Laura
were waiting for him to open it.

Conor tore the paper off
and ripped open the box.
He smiled.

He began to jump
up and down.

'A cowboy suit!' he shouted.
'**Wow**!'

He put the chaps on first.
They had fringes
all down the sides.

Then he put on the waistcoat.
It had three shiny buttons
and a little pocket
on each side.

He knotted the scarf
around his neck.
He put the hat on his head
and tipped it back
out of his eyes.

'Howdy, Maw,' he said.
'Howdy, Sis.'
Mum and Laura laughed.

He buckled on the gunbelt
and pulled the guns
out of their holsters.

'Stick 'em up!' he shouted at Dad.
'Don't shoot!' Dad screamed,
putting his hands up.

It was the best day ever.

That night, Conor
did not want to take off
his new cowboy suit.
In the end, he took it off,
and put his pyjamas on.

Then he put the cowboy suit
back on –
over his pyjamas.

All night long he had
cowboy dreams.

It was the best night ever.

In the morning,
Dad called him for school.

Conor took off the cowboy suit
and his pyjamas,
and put on his school clothes.
Then he put on
the cowboy suit –
over his school clothes.

He went down to the kitchen.
'Howdy, all!' he said.

They all stopped eating.
They stared at Conor.
'You can't wear that
to school,' said Laura.
'Conor, I think you should
leave it at home,' said Dad.
'Conor, I really –' said Mum.'

'I'm wearing it to school,'
said Conor. 'It's brilliant!'

'But –' said Mum, Dad
and Laura.

'One more word and
I'll shoot!' said Conor.

'They'll all laugh at you,'
said Laura.

Cowboy Con
just crunched his cornflakes.

Mum drove Conor and Laura
to school.
Laura was wearing her uniform.
All the other children were
wearing their uniforms.

'Take it off, Conor,
before we get out of the car,'
Laura said.
'Nope!' said Conor.

Mum handed Conor
his schoolbag and lunch.
'Are you sure you don't
want me to mind the
cowboy suit for you?' she asked.

'See you at sundown, Maw,'
said Conor.

Lots of children stared at Conor.
'Going to a fancy dress party?'
they shouted.

Cowboy Con walked right on.

He reached his classroom door.
He fixed his hat.
He put his hands
near the holsters,
just in case.

He strode into the classroom.

All the children looked up
and stopped talking.
They all stared.

'Howdy!' said Conor.

Conor walked to his desk,
nice and slow.
His heels clicked
on the hard floor.
He took off his schoolbag
and put it away.

Then he took off his hat
and hung it on the back
of his chair.

'Mornin', Ma'am,'
he said to the teacher.
Ms Keane stared.
'Eh ... eh ...'

Conor flashed her a huge smile.
'Just call me **Cowboy Con**,'
he said.

At break time, Cowboy Con
strolled out into the yard.
Lots of children wanted
to play with him.

'Yee haw!' they yelled,
rounding up the cattle.
'Giddy-up.'
It was great fun.

They all wanted to try on
his cowboy suit.

'Nope,' said Conor.
'Bring your own, pardner.'

Ms Keane heard him.

Oh no, she thought.
Tomorrow I'll have
twenty-five cowboys
in my class.
What will I do?

Conor's friends, Sarah and
Kevin and Mark, all said they
would dress up tomorrow.

'I'll come as a fairy,' said Sarah.
'I have a beautiful fairy dress.'

'I have a cool dancing outfit,'
said Mark.
'**You do**?' they all said.
Mark told them that
he wanted to be in a boy band
when he was older.

But other boys laughed at him
for learning dancing
so he never talked about it.
'I love dancing,' he said.
'You can see my outfit
tomorrow.'

Kevin had a gladiator outfit.
'It has great boots,
and a shiny helmet,'
he told them.

Ms Keane heard all the plans.
During break,
she had a chat with Conor.

After break,
she got Conor
to make an announcement.

'Tomorrow is Friday,'
Conor said.
'Every Friday from now on
we can all **dress up**.'

The children cheered.
'Hurray for Cowboy Con,'
they all said.
'This is fun.'

Conor told Mum
and Dad and Laura
all about it that night.

'That's not fair,' said Laura,
'I want to dress up too.'

'Wear your magician's outfit
to school, then,'
said Conor.
'Maybe I will,' said Laura.

And next morning – she did!

That day, Conor's class
was full of strange people.

There was Cowboy Con,
of course.

There was Mark,
the fantastic
dancer.

There was Sarah,
the beautiful fairy.

And Kevin,
the gladiator.

There were:

devils

angels

monkeys

pilots

and pirates.

57

And at the top of the class was:

THE SHERIFF.

They all had the best day ever.
Even Ms Keane!

In Laura's class there was
one magician –
and everybody else was
in uniform.
But at break time
they started to plan.
'**We'll** dress up on Fridays, too,'
they said.

'It was all Conor's idea,'
said Laura.

'You're a great brother,'
she told him later.
'A cool dude.'

Conor blew the smoke
from the tip of his gun.

He tipped his hat.

'Gee, thank you, Sis,' he said.
'It's been a real pleasure.'